BREAKAWAY!

The History of Hockey

Jaime Winters

CRABTREE
Publishing Company
www.crabtreebooks.com

Author: Jaime Winters

Publishing plan research and development: Reagan Miller, Crabtree Publishing Company

Editors: Joanne Randolph, Kelly Spence

Proofreader: Wendy Scavuzzo

Photo research: Melissa McClellan

Cover Design: Samara Parent

Design: T. J. Choleva

Prepress technician: Samara Parent

Print and production coordinator: Katherine Berti

Consultant
Ross Firmin, Hamilton Minor Hockey Council

Developed and produced for Crabtree Publishing by BlueAppleWorks Inc.

Images on cover (clockwise from top): Ottawa Senators, Stanley Cup Champions, 1911; Scoring great, Phil Esposito, center for the Boston Bruins; "Mr. Hockey," Gordie Howe, captain of the Detroit Red Wings

Image on title page: Gore Bay women's hockey team of Manitoulin Island, Ontario, 1921

Illustration: Carlyn Iverson (p 18 bottom)

Photographs
Front Cover: Thinkstock: (bottom right)
Wikimedia Commons: (top cener, bottom left, bottom center, bottom right)

Interior: Shutterstock.com: © B Calkins (page toppers); © Shooter Bob Square Lenses (hand & puck); © Iurii Osadchi (p 4, 5 top, 5 bottom, 25, 26–27 bottom); © photosthatrock (p 15, 17); © lsantilli (p 19); © Sven Hoppe (p 26–27 top); © lev radin (p 28); © Corepics VOF(p 29 top); © Pavel L Photo and Video (p 30) **Dreamstime.com:** © Ron Chapple (p 7 bottom)
Public Domain: Conn Smythe Fonds (TOC, p 12–13 top); p 6–7 top; George Catlin (p 6–7 bottom); Seth Eastman (p 7 top right);Arthur Farrell (p 8); Musée McCord Museum (p 9 top); William Notman & Son (p 9 bottom, p 12–13 bottom, p 16); Alexander Henderson (p 10); p 11 top; Topley Studio Fonds (p 11 bottom); Edward F Dolan (p 12 left, p 18); p 13 right; p 14; p 19 top; Royal Collection (p 20 left); p 21 middle, bottom, right; p 22; Byron Harmon (p 23 top); Preston Rivulettes (p 23); p 24
Keystone Press: © Al Charest (p 27 left); © Aftonbladet/Ibl Bildbyr (p 27 right)
Creative Commons: Sologoal (p 7 bottom right); Fanthomas (p 20–21 top); Bundesarchiv, Bild 102-05472(p 26 bottom)

Library and Archives Canada Cataloguing in Publication

Winters, Jaime, author
Breakaway! : the history of hockey / Jaime Winters.

(Hockey source)
Includes index.
Issued in print and electronic formats.
ISBN 978-0-7787-0752-3 (bound).--ISBN 978-0-7787-0780-6 (pbk.).--
ISBN 978-1-4271-7680-6 (pdf).--ISBN 978-1-4271-7676-9 (html)

1. Hockey--History--Juvenile literature. I. Title.

GV846.5.W56 2014 j796.96209 C2014-903828-3
C2014-903829-1

Library of Congress Cataloging-in-Publication Data

CIP available at the Library of Congress

Crabtree Publishing Company

www.crabtreebooks.com 1-800-387-7650

Printed in the U.S.A./092014/JA20140811

 In Canada: We acknowledge the financial support of the Government of Canada through the Canada Book Fund for our publishing activities.

Published in Canada
Crabtree Publishing
616 Welland Ave.
St. Catharines, ON
L2M 5V6

Published in the United States
Crabtree Publishing
PMB 59051
350 Fifth Avenue, 59th Floor
New York, New York 10118

Published in the United Kingdom
Crabtree Publishing
Maritime House
Basin Road North, Hove
BN41 1WR

Published in Australia
Crabtree Publishing
3 Charles Street
Coburg North
VIC 3058

TABLE OF CONTENTS

The Fastest Game on Earth 4

The Birth of Hockey 6

The North American Game 8

A Growing Interest 10

The Rise of the NHL 12

The Game Goes Pro 14

Getting into Gear 16

Goalie's Armor 18

Hockey in Europe 20

Women in Hockey 22

Girls Got Game! 24

The World Rink 26

All Kinds of Hockey 28

Hockey Around the World 30

Learning More 31

Glossary and Index 32

HOCKEY Source

LET'S PLAY HOCKEY!

THE FASTEST GAME ON EARTH

With speed, skill, and nonstop action, hockey is one of the world's most popular sports—and one of its fastest! With pucks flying at speeds up to 100 miles (161 km) per hour, it's easy to see why hockey is called the fastest game on the planet. Some players zoom down the ice at up to 27 miles (43.5 km) per hour. Fans everywhere love watching their favorite players and teams battle for the puck.

Game of Rivalries

Fierce **rivalries** make hockey one of the world's most exciting spectator sports, especially in North America. Not only are Canada and the U.S.A. long-standing rivals in men's hockey, they are **archrivals** in women's hockey, too. Fans went wild when the teams faced off for gold at the 2014 Sochi Olympics.

The U.S.A. and Canada are the top women's hockey teams in the world. Sparks flew when they met at the 2014 Olympics.

A Nail-biter

Canada took home gold in both men's and women's hockey at Sochi. The women's final especially had fans on the edges of their seats. With less than four minutes remaining in the game, the U.S.A. was winning 2-0. Canada had yet to score, but, in a shocking turnaround, the Canadians tied it up with two goals in the final minutes. Eight minutes into **sudden-death** play, Canada scored again to win the gold!

The Canadian women's ice hockey team show off their gold medals after their match against the U.S. team at the 2014 Olympics.

Cool Fact!

In 2014, Phil and Amanda Kessel became the first brother and sister to play for the U.S. women's and men's Olympic hockey teams.

Disappointed, But Not Defeated

Losing the gold medal game at the 2014 Olympics was heartbreaking. The U.S. women's team had given the game their all and believed they would win. However, they didn't lose their team spirit. "...we still have belief in each other and how proud we are. That defines us," said forward Julie Chu. "Not just one game."

An emotional Julie Chu receives her silver medal. She was chosen to be the flag bearer for Team U.S.A. at the Olympics' closing ceremony.

THE BIRTH OF HOCKEY

Hockey has a long history. Clay tablets more than 5,000 years old were found in Iraq. They tell the story of a great warrior king named Gilgamesh who played a hockey-like game called Pukku-Mikku. The game was played with a curved stick, or "mikku," and a hollow wooden ring, or "pukku."

Play Like an Egyptian

An ancient Greek sculpture (514 BC) shows figures playing a hockey-like game with sticks. Two opponents are even shown facing off for a ball. However, other archaeological evidence shows that the popular game may have come from Egypt, where people played a similar game more than 4,000 years ago.

This ancient Greek sculpture shows young people using curved sticks to move a ball in a game similar to modern hockey.

Hurling and Shinty

In the 1200s, the Irish played a game called hurling. They used a curved tree branch to "carry" a stone, or cow dropping, across a field and hurl it into their opponents' goal. It is still very popular in Ireland and around the world. The Scots played a similar game called shinty. In North America, native people played their own ball-and-stick games, sometimes on ice. When Irish and Scottish newcomers arrived in the 1700s and 1800s, they brought hurling and shinty with them and began playing these games on ice, too.

In North America, native people played their own ball-and-stick games, often on ice during winters.

From 100 to 1,000 men from opposing villages gathered to play ball-and-stick games together (above) as witnessed and painted by artist George Catlin in the 1850s.

Cool Fact!

The name hockey may come from "hoquet," the French word for shepherd's crook, or "hoghee," the Iroquois word for tree branch or the pain from being whacked by a tree branch.

Shinty is one of the early forms of ice hockey. Canadians still call pick-up, or informal games of hockey, shinny.

THE NORTH AMERICAN GAME

Playing hockey on frozen ponds and rivers became popular in North America in the 1800s. The game didn't look much like it does today, though. Teams often had as many as 20 to 30 players each. The puck was often a wooden stopper from a barrel and, when it was shot wide of the goal, it often got lost in a snowbank.

Born in My Backyard

Not one, not two, but three cities claim to be the birthplace of the first modern hockey game. Legend has it that modern hockey was born on Long Pond in Windsor, Nova Scotia, around 1810. Another legend says it was born in Halifax, Nova Scotia, in 1850. Still another says it was born on Kingston Harbour in Kingston, Ontario, in 1855.

This drawing is from the first book ever written about ice hockey. The book, published in 1899, was called Canada's Royal Winter Game *by Arthur Farrell.*

From the Pond to the Rink

Wherever modern hockey was born, the first indoor game was played at Victoria Skating Rink in Montreal, Quebec, in 1875. Teams had nine players each. Instead of a ball, they used a flat disk-shaped piece of wood, which was less likely to fly off into the crowd. Two years later, the *Montreal Gazette* printed rules of the game that teams everywhere began to follow. The rules included no forward passing, set the number of players to seven per team, and also required goalies to stay on their feet at all times.

At the time it was built, the Victoria Skating Rink was considered "one of the finest covered rinks in the world."

No boards stood between the ice and the crowd in the Victoria Skating Rink in Montreal, Quebec. The rink was built for skating, not hockey.

A GROWING INTEREST

In the 1880s, people from all over Canada and the U.S. traveled to Quebec for the Montreal Winter Carnival. This winter festival included skating balls, winter sports, and even a giant ice palace made of 10,000 ice blocks! When hockey first appeared there in 1883, the game was a breakaway hit that found many fans. Hockey **leagues** began springing up across Canada and the U.S.

A crowd of hockey fans gather outside to watch a hockey game at the 1893 Montreal Winter Carnival. By 1895, Montreal alone was home to more than 100 hockey teams.

Sport of Nations

The Montreal AAA won the first Stanley Cup championship in 1893.

In 1885, hockey leagues formed in Kingston, Ontario, and Montreal, Quebec. At the time, ice polo played with a ball instead of a puck was popular in the U.S. However, when hockey games were played at Yale University in New Haven, Connecticut, and John Hopkins University in Baltimore, Maryland, in 1893, hockey's popularity overtook ice polo. In 1896, the first U.S. hockey league formed in New York City. Not long after, the first International Amateur Championship between Canada and the U.S. was held there.

Lord Stanley Loves Hockey

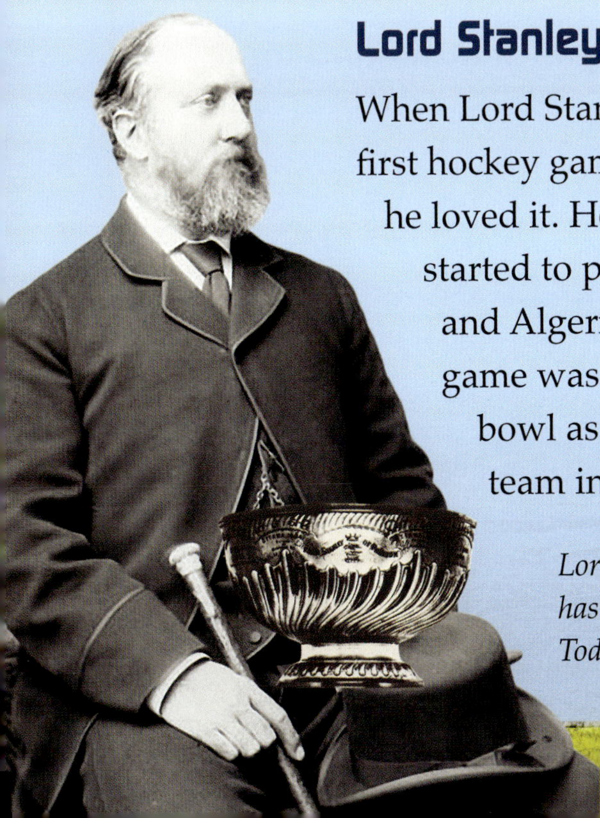

When Lord Stanley, the Governor General of Canada, saw his first hockey game at the Montreal Winter Carnival in 1889, he loved it. He built an ice rink at his house in Ottawa and started to play the game himself. So did his sons Arthur and Algernon, and daughter Isobel. Four years later, the game was so popular that Lord Stanley donated a silver bowl as a challenge cup to be won by the champion team in Canada. With that, the Stanley Cup was born.

Lord Stanley and the original Stanley Cup. Hockey has no greater glory than winning the Stanley Cup. Today, pro teams fight tooth and stick for it.

THE RISE OF THE NHL

Not all the leagues could survive. Some folded, or split up, some joined together, and some even formed new leagues despite disagreements and restructuring by team owners.

Go West Young Player

Ambrose O'Brien was a businessman who, with his father M.J. O'Brien, owned the Renfrew Millionaires. In 1909, the Eastern Canada Hockey League (ECHL) refused to accept his bid to join the league. O'Brien fought back by forming the National Hockey Association (NHA) on the ECHL's turf. The NHA made changes to the rules to make the game more exciting. These changes included cutting down the number of players from seven to six, which made games faster and more exciting. They also changed the number of periods of play from two 30-minute periods to three 20-minute periods. This gave players more time to recharge and fans more time to buy soda, popcorn, and candy. Even with all these exciting changes, the Pacific Coast Hockey Association (PCHA), which had also formed in 1909, was still able to lure talented players to play out west.

Joe Hall was a Canadian ***professional*** *ice hockey player, who played for the Quebec Bulldogs, winning the Stanley Cup twice with that team. Hall was* ***inducted*** *into the Hockey Hall of Fame in 1961.*

One League to Rule Them All

In 1917, bickering team owners tore apart the NHA and formed the National Hockey League (NHL) out of the shreds. The new league competed for players and the Stanley Cup with the PCHA and the Western Canada Hockey League (WCHL) in the prairies.

In 1924, the NHL expanded into the U.S. with the addition of the Boston Bruins and the PCHA folded. Even though fans packed PCHA games, the owners were going broke maintaining arenas that were empty the rest of the time. By 1926, three more American teams joined the NHL, which was the only league left. The WCHL had folded because it couldn't pay for top players. Since then, only NHL teams have been allowed to compete for the Stanley Cup.

The Boston Bruins were the first U.S. hockey team to join the NHL.

Cool Fact!

In December 1917, Dave Ritchie, defenseman of the Montreal Wanderers, scored the NHL's first goal in the first minute of the league's first game.

THE GAME GOES PRO

As the NHL evolved, so did the game. Hockey players went from being **amateur** athletes to pros who were paid top dollar to play the game.

All Play and No Pay

Unlike pro athletes, amateurs are not paid to play sports. When hockey first started, all the players were amateurs. They played hockey for the love of it and worked at jobs to make a living. Early hockey superstar Fred Taylor turned down an offer to play for the Toronto Marlboroughs when he was 18 for lack of money. Playing for the Marlboroughs would have meant moving from Listowel, where he worked in a piano factory adding $20 a month to his family's income.

When he turned down the Toronto Marlboroughs offer, Fred "Cyclone" Taylor was banned from playing anywhere in Ontario. A year later, he left home to play in Manitoba and became a scoring superstar.

Cool Fact!

While today's pros play for the Stanley Cup, amateurs play for the Allan Cup.

Money Talks, Players Walk

As team owners profited from charging admission to games and leagues competed for top players who could draw fans to the games, things began to change. Some teams paid players with gifts, such as $5 pairs of skates. Others secretly paid them cash and gave them paying day jobs as well. In 1904, the first pro hockey league sprang up in the U.S. Once it lured Canadian superstars to play for pay, there was no stopping hockey from going pro.

Sidney Crosby of the Pittsburgh Penguins made around $12 million during the 2013–14 season.

Show Me the Money

1904 IHL* Minimum Pay	$15–40 a week
1904 IHL Player/Rink Manager Pay**	$1,800 a year
1970 NHL Average Pay	$18,000 a year
1980 NHL Average Pay	$100,000 a year
2012 NHL Average Pay	$2.4 million a year

* International Hockey League—the first pro league

** When defenseman Hod Stuart signed with the first pro league in Michigan—the International Hockey League—he negotiated a salary to play and to manage the rink. Fred "Cyclone" Taylor joined the IHL for more than $3,000 per season.

GETTING INTO GEAR

As the game changed from amateur to pro, so did the equipment. Street clothes no longer cut it on the ice. Hockey gear evolved to protect players from the **hazards** of the game.

Suiting Up

In the 1800s, hockey players had no gear except skates and a stick. Early skates were just a pair of shoes with blades strapped to them. They battled to win games in their street clothes. But it wasn't long before players began strapping thick catalogs and books to their shins to shield them from blows from the puck. Today, players wear crack-resistant plastic shinpads, waterproof padded hockey pants, shoulder pads, padded gloves, groin protectors, mouth guards, and helmets to protect their bodies like a suit of armor.

Early hockey players often got hurt while playing hockey, since they did not wear any protective clothing.

Sticky Weapons

Early sticks were made from carved tree branches. Over time, aluminum, then graphite and **Kevlar**, were used to make sticks. Today, modern sticks allow players to release quicker and harder shots in the heat of the battle. Nevertheless, stickmakers and players continue to search for the perfect stick.

With all their new gear and high-tech sticks, today's hockey players can shoot pucks at very high speeds. The record set in a skills competion is 110.3 mph (177.5 kmph).

Tape It Up

In the 1920s, players began taping their sticks. The tape improved their grip on the shaft and strengthened the blade. Today, some players even use black tape on the blade to make it hard for goalies to see the puck on their stick.

Cool Fact!

Hockey pucks were not always made of rubber the way they are today. Some of the first pucks were made from stones, lumps of coal, and even frozen cow droppings!

GOALIE'S ARMOR

No player is as grateful as the goalie for the development of protective hockey gear. After all, a goalie may face as many as 80 shots a game!

Goalies Suit Up

Early goaltenders did not wear added padding or protective gear. Injuries were common since goalies tried to block shots with their stick, hands, feet, and other body parts. In the 1890s, some began wearing leather goal pads from the game of cricket. As shooters began lifting the puck, goalies borrowed chest protectors from baseball. Once the rules changed allowing goalies to drop to their knees to stop shots, goal pads developed to protect their knees and keep them dry. Goalies also invented the blocker and catching glove to protect their hands and help stop shots. Today, they cover more of the net than ever just by suiting up for the game.

Clint Benedict wore the first mask in a game in 1930. He had a broken nose that he wanted to protect. The only problem was the mask made it difficult to see the puck.

The Men Behind the Mask

In 1959, Jacques Plante took a shot in the face that required 200 stitches. He refused to return to the game without a mask. Soon after, all goalies wore masks.

In the 1972 series between Canada and Russia, Vladislav Tretiak wore a helmet with a birdcage type of mask. When Tretiak stopped Canada's shooters like a brick wall, birdcage masks became popular.

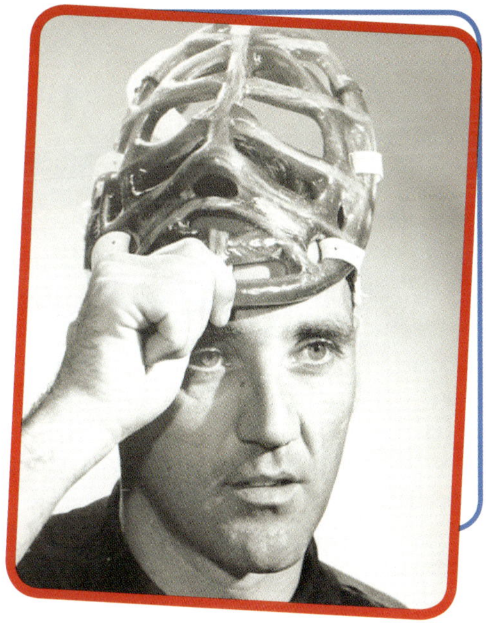

After getting hurt in goal, Jacques Plante was the first NHL goaltender to wear a mask during every game. He came up with and tested many different mask designs.

The puck moves at very high speeds. The goaltender wears special equipment to stay safe and to help him or her stop pucks from getting into the net.

HOCKEY IN EUROPE

Lord Stanley never saw a game played for his Cup. When his brother died in 1893, he and his family had to return to England. However, they brought their love of the game across the ocean with them.

The Stanleys vs. The Royals

In 1895, an extremely cold winter blasted England with snow and ice. The lake at Buckingham Palace froze over and Lord Stanley's sons convinced the Royal family to play a game of hockey. Lord Stanley and five of his sons hit the ice against six members of the royal court, including the future King George V. Legend has it that the royal court scored once while the Stanley brothers scored so many times that, out of respect, they stopped keeping score. Nevertheless, the royal family became fans of the game and watched the Stanley brothers crush several teams outside the palace, too.

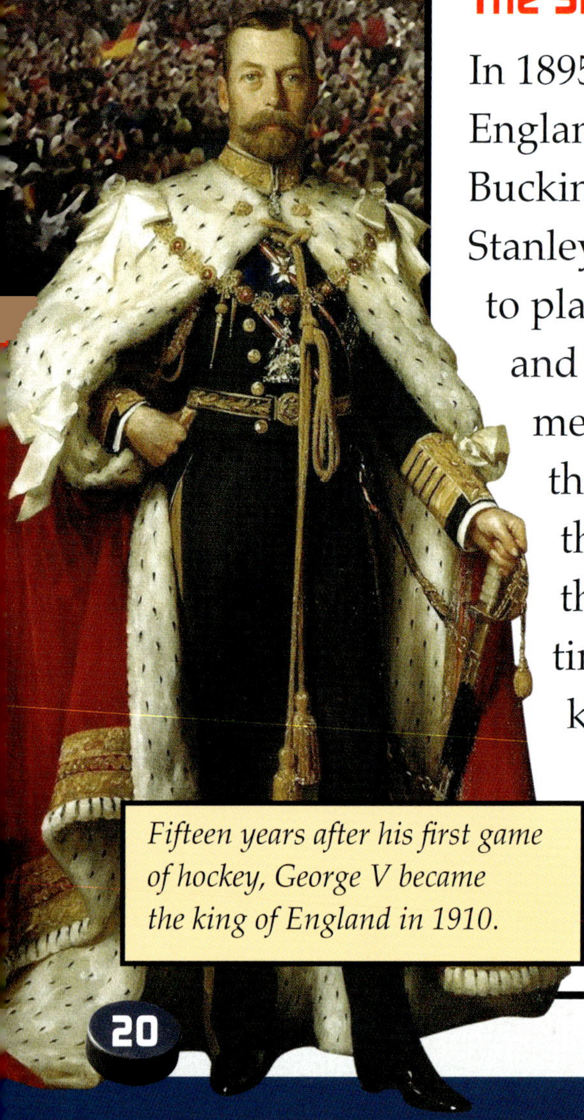

Fifteen years after his first game of hockey, George V became the king of England in 1910.

A League of Its Own

Wherever the Stanley brothers played, their skill and enthusiasm increased interest in hockey. By 1903, Europe had a league of five teams. In 1908, the Ligue Internationale de Hockey sur Glace was born to run international competitions. Two years later, England won the first European championship. Eventually, the Ligue became the International Ice Hockey Federation (IIHF) that governs the sport around the world today.

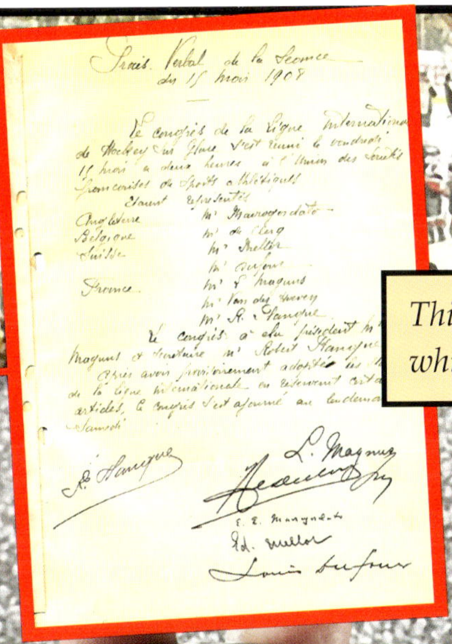

This is the LIHG/IIHF founding document, which was signed on May 15, 1908.

Great Britain's hockey team played in the European Championships held at Davos, Switzerland, in 1926.

Cool Fact!

The IIHF has 70 members from around the world, and it runs the world championships for junior, men's, and women's hockey.

WOMEN IN HOCKEY

Men and women often played together in the just-for-fun games on frozen ponds and rivers, where hockey's earliest stars were born.

Lord Stanley's 14-year-old daughter Isobel played with her brothers on the rink her father had built at their house. She also started the first women's hockey team.

A Team of Their Own

Isobel Stanley and her Government House team played against the Rideau Ladies in 1889. They played in long wool skirts, turtleneck sweaters, and big hats. Women often used their ankle-length skirts to full advantage. Forwards hid the puck in their skirts as they moved down the ice, and goalies stopped the puck with them. Other players even crouched in front of the goalie and draped their skirts across the front of the net to block shots.

This is the earliest known photograph of women playing hockey, taken at Rideau Hall, Ottawa, in 1890. Isobel Stanley, Lord Stanley's daughter, is wearing the lighter dress.

Women Rock the Game

Around 1900, women's hockey leagues popped up in eastern and western Canada and as far north as Dawson City in the Yukon. Though not everyone thought women should play such a rough-and-tumble game, that didn't stop competitive women's hockey from becoming popular in Canada and the U.S. in the 1920s. Both men and women went to games. However, women's hockey didn't receive the same money, equipment, and opportunities as men's and began to lose popularity in the 1940s.

In the 1920s, the Vancouver Amazons played in a tournament with the Seattle Vamps. Some people say this was the first international women's hockey competition.

From 1930-1940, the Preston Rivulettes played about 350 games. They tied 3, lost 2, and won the rest!

GIRLS GOT GAME!

In the 1980s, women's hockey made a comeback. More girls and women in North America took up the game than ever before, and a new era of organized women's hockey began.

She Shoots! She Scores!

By 1990, women's hockey was the hottest story on ice. The first international women's hockey tournament took place during March in Ottawa, Canada. Nearly 85 journalists showed up to cover the action. The players were thrilled with the chance to compete against the best teams from Sweden, Finland, Norway, West Germany, Switzerland, and Japan. Canada and the U.S. made it to the championship game. The U.S. scored two goals first and Canada roared back with five goals straight to win. What's more, women's hockey scored big with fans around the world.

Susana Yuen celebrates with her teammates after winning the 1990 World Women's Championship in Ottawa, defeating the U.S.

Have Skills, Will Play

Women also infiltrated the men's game and the Olympics. In 1992, goalie Manon Rheaume played goalie for the Tampa Bay Lightning in pre-season exhibition games, becoming the first woman to play in a pro men's league. In 1998, women's hockey teams got their first chance to compete at the Nagano Olympics in Japan when women's hockey became an official sport of the Games.

The National Women's Hockey League was established in 2000 and has since split into the Canadian Women's Hockey League and the Western Women's Hockey League.

Faster Play

No **body checking** is allowed in women's hockey. Many fans say this makes women's hockey faster and more exciting than men's hockey.

Cool Fact!

Hayley Wickenheiser became the first woman to score a goal in men's pro hockey when she joined a Finnish men's team in 2003.

THE WORLD RINK

The first world championship of hockey was held at the 1920 Summer Olympics. The event was for men only. Today, the world hockey championships are an important event. Both men and women have the chance to compete in it, as well as the Olympics.

The World Championships

This competition is the top international hockey tournament that happens every year. Since 1977, the world championships have been open to all players—amateurs and pros. Games are played on a larger rink than NHL games. Some rules also vary from the NHL. For example, in the NHL, players who fight receive **penalties**. In the world championships, players who fight are thrown out of the game.

Canada takes to the ice to play Sweden at the 1928 Olympics in St. Moritz, Switzerland. Canada won the gold medal and Sweden the silver medal.

The Olympic Games

The Olympic Games take place once every four years. In 1988, a rule change allowed pro athletes to compete at the Olympics for the first time. However, it wasn't until 1998 that the NHL changed its schedule to allow its players to play at the Olympics. That was the same year that women's hockey became an Olympic sport. Like the world championships, the size of the rink and some rules vary from the NHL for Olympic competition.

At the 2014 Olympics, Canada's men's team won the gold medal. Sweden won the silver medal, and Finland took home the bronze.

ALL KINDS OF HOCKEY

Ice hockey is only one of many different kinds of hockey. There is also street hockey, field hockey, and sledge hockey, which is also played on ice.

Street and Field

When roads were first paved in North America around 1900, street hockey was born. People took to the streets to play hockey on their feet with a ball or puck. Later, when roller skates and in-line skates hit the streets, players strapped them on and roller and in-line hockey began. Today, street hockey is also called road hockey as well as dek hockey because it's often played indoors on a deck-like surface. Field hockey, which began around the 1800s, is played on a grass or turf field.

Street hockey is common in many countries around the world. Many hockey players get their start playing street hockey, or play street hockey when they don't have access to ice.

Sledge Hockey

Two players invented sledge hockey in Sweden in the 1960s, when they didn't want to give up playing hockey due to physical disabilities. Players sit on a sled, or sledge, with two metal blades under the seat and a stick in each hand. Both sticks are used to propel the sledge around the ice, as well as shoot and stickhandle the puck. In 1994, sledge hockey became an official sport at the **Paralympic Games**. Since then, it's become one of the Games' most popular events.

The United States beat England in the 2014 Field Hockey World Cup. In field hockey, sticks are J-shaped and are flat on one side and curved on the other.

In the 2014 Paralympic Games gold medal match in Sochi, Russia, the U.S players celebrate a goal.

HOCKEY AROUND THE WORLD

Hockey is popular around the world. The Olympics and pro hockey, especially the NHL playoffs for the Stanley Cup, excite the minds and hearts of fans everywhere. The Internet is also making it easier for fans and players to connect with each other.

Future Superstars

Children and adults play the game in local recreational, community, and school leagues all over the world. Little leagues and hockey camps provide opportunities for children to learn hockey skills while having fun playing the game. Tournaments, such as the Junior World Championships, allow young players to emerge and develop into future superstars who will set the ice on fire.

LEARNING MORE

Check out these books and websites to find out more about the fastest game on Earth.

Books

The Best of Everything Hockey Book (The All-Time Best of Sports) by Shane Frederick, Capstone Press, 2011

The Hilarious History of Hockey by Helaine Becker, Scholastic Canada Ltd., 2010

Inside Hockey: The Legends, Facts, and Feats That Made the Game by Keltie Thomas, Maple Tree Press, 2008

Sports Illustrated The Hockey Book, by Editors of Sports Illustrated, Sports Illustrated Books, 2010

Websites

NHL.com for Kids

The NHL site for kids features photos, videos, games, and information about their special programs for kids.

www.nhl.com/kids/

Hockey Hall of Fame

The Hockey Hall of Fame has information about the best hockey players of the past and present.

www.hhof.com

GLOSSARY

amateur Someone who does something without pay

archrivals Main rivals, or someone who tries to beat someone else at something often

body checking In hockey, intentional body contact to try to stop an opponent or take possession of the puck

hazards Dangers

inducted Admitted or voted in as a new member

Kevlar A brand of human-made fabric that is very strong and thick

leagues Group of sports teams that play against one another

Paralympic Games An international sporting event for individuals with disabilities

penalties Punishments for breaking a rule

professional Someone who is paid for what he or she does

rivalries Competitions or struggles between two people or teams to see which ones are the best

sudden death Used to break a tie at the end of a game, play continues and ends when either team scores

INDEX

amateur 14, 16, 32
Benedict, Clint 18
Chu, Julie 5
Crosby, Sidney 15
Eastern Canada Hockey League (ECHL) 12
field hockey 28
First Nations 7
gear 16, 17, 18
goalies 18, 22, 25
International Ice Hockey Federation (IIHF) 21
Kessel, Amanda 5
Kessel, Phil 5
National Hockey Association (NHA) 12, 13
National Hockey League (NHL) 3, 12, 13, 14, 15, 19, 26, 27, 30
Olympics 4, 5, 25, 26, 27, 30
Pacific Coast Hockey Association (PCHA) 12, 13
Paralympics 29
penalties 26
Plante, Jacques 19
Pukku-Mikku 6
Rheaume, Manon 25
Shinty 7
sledge hockey 28, 29
Stanley Cup 11, 14, 30
Stanley, Lord 11, 20, 22
sticks 6, 17, 29
street hockey 28
Toronto Marlboroughs 14
Tretiak, Vladislav 19
Wickenheiser, Hayley 25
Yuen, Susana 24